Rescue & Jessica
A Life-Changing Friendship

Jessica Kensky *and* Patrick Downes

illustrated by Scott Magoon

WALKER BOOKS
AND SUBSIDIARIES

LONDON · BOSTON · SYDNEY · AUCKLAND

On a special farm in the countryside, a pup named Rescue was in training. He was learning to help people who could not see. But he was worried.

His trainer had just said, "You aren't meant to be a guide dog."

That was hard for Rescue to hear. Helping people who can't see was the family business.

"The service dog team is better for you," his trainer said. "Service dogs work *beside* their partners, instead of in front of them."

Will I be a good service dog? Rescue wondered.

What will my new partner be like?

Will she like me?

Rescue didn't want to let anyone down.

In a hospital in the city, a girl named Jessica was worried.

Both of her legs were badly hurt. Everyone hoped her right leg would heal, but the doctors had to remove part of her left leg so she could be healthy again.

"You're an amputee now, Jessica," the doctor explained. "You have to wear a prosthetic leg or use a wheelchair for the rest of your life."

That was hard to hear. She had only ever walked on her own two legs.

How will I do things on my own? Jessica wondered.

When will I be able to walk again?

What will my life be like?

Her whole family was worried about her, and she didn't want to let anyone down.

Good boy.

Back in the countryside, Rescue was learning how to be a service dog.

When he wore his blue cape, that meant he was in training.

He had to stay by his partner's side.

He fetched all kinds of things.

He even learned how to open doors.

"Rescue, you're a natural!" said his trainer.

At the hospital, Jessica was learning new ways to do things that used to come easily.

She used a wheelchair to get around.

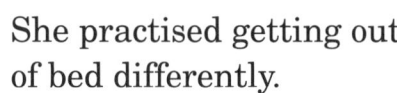

She practised getting out of bed differently.

She put on a prosthetic leg so she could stand.

She was learning how to walk again, even though her right leg still hurt.

"Jessica, you are becoming strong," said her doctors.

Rescue was proud of all he had accomplished, but he still worried.

He was named in honour of a brave firefighter.

He had big shoes to fill.

Rescue wanted to help people, just like his namesake.

Jessica knew she had made a lot of progress, but she was frustrated and sad about the things she still couldn't do.

She wondered if she would ever be happy again.

She felt like the changes were too big, too much.

One day, a visitor came to see Jessica and she brought her service dog, Currahee. Jessica saw how a smart dog like Currahee could help her. That very day, she started filling out the application to ask for a dog of her own.

HOSPITAL DIRECTORY

SURGICAL FLOORS
INFECTIOUS DISEASES
EMERGENCY
INFUSION CENTER
ICU
AUDITORIUM

ADMINISTR

MEDICAL FLOORS
CARDIOLOGY
HEM   ONCOLOGY
REH
MED   RARY

HECK IN

After a while, Jessica got some very exciting news.

Rescue got exciting news, too. He also got
a new red cape.

Finally, the big day arrived.

"It's nice to meet you, Rescue," said Jessica.

She looks so nice and so pretty, Rescue thought.

Rescue stood up very tall. He hoped she didn't notice his legs were trembling.

But his wagging tail gave him away.

Jessica smiled a big smile and laughed a big laugh for the first time in a long time.

Jessica and Rescue stayed in the countryside for a few weeks, and Rescue showed her all the things he could do.

Ring! Ring! Ring!

"You're amazing!" Jessica told Rescue.

You think I'm *amazing?* Rescue thought. *I think* you're *amazing!*

Back in the city, Rescue and Jessica got used to working together.

Rescue brought her the things she needed.

He opened things that were hard for her to reach.

Rescue barked if Jessica needed someone.

If she tripped, he would hold steady so she could get back up.

Rescue and Jessica were always together, but when she didn't need his help, Rescue *really* liked to sleep.

Jessica knew that even though Rescue was special, he was a regular dog, too. She made sure that Rescue had playtime every day.

But Jessica still wasn't completely healthy. One day, her doctor told her that her right leg would have to be removed, too. She would need to wear two prosthetic legs. This didn't get any easier for Jessica to hear.

The night after the doctor removed her right leg, Rescue knew just what to do to help Jessica, all on his own.

Rescue and Jessica had to start all over again.

Slowly but surely, they learned how to do all the things they needed to do.

Together.

They did chores together,

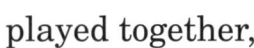
played together,

and snuggled together.

For the first time in a long time, Jessica felt happy.

And that made Rescue happy, too.

"You changed my life, Rescue," she said.
"I couldn't have done this without you."

I'm so proud of us, he thought.

"You rescued me, Rescue," said Jessica.

But the truth was, they had rescued each other.

AUTHORS' NOTE

Rescue and Jessica's story is based on a real-life friendship. Jessica Kensky was injured in the 2013 Boston Marathon bombing, and she eventually became a double amputee. She received a black Labrador named Rescue to help her learn how to live her new life. Rescue was named in honour of Massachusetts firefighter Jon Davies, who rode on the truck known as Rescue 1. He gave his life in the line of duty on December 8, 2011. Jessica and her husband Patrick Downes, who is also an amputee from the bombing, consider Rescue their best friend and couldn't imagine their lives without him. Though Jessica was an adult when she met Rescue, much of this story is true.

Service dogs like Rescue come in all different breeds and sizes. They spend years in training so they can do things to help people that regular pets can't do. Service dogs, also known as assistance dogs, can help their partners with seeing, hearing and socializing. They help their partners do everyday things like open doors, turn on lights and fetch items that are out of reach. They can even find the phone to call for help if their partner has an emergency.

Rescue was trained through a U.S. organization called NEADS (National Education for Assistance Dogs). In the UK, there are many charities that, like NEADS, train dogs to become assistance dogs. All accredited charities become members of Assistance Dogs UK, an organization that helps to ensure assistance dogs meet high standards of training and are well cared for.

To learn more about NEADS and Assistance Dogs UK, visit www.neads.org and www.assistancedogs.org.uk.

ACKNOWLEDGEMENTS

Our dear friend and agent Clelia Gore, you inspired and worked with us to bring this story to life, and your visionary spirit and limitless talent made this book possible. Katie Cunningham, Allison Cole, Ann Stott, and everyone at Candlewick Press, the instant connection we shared has grown into a relationship that has brought us so much joy and creativity. We have savoured every moment with you. Rescue is forever indebted to you for all the care packages. Scott Magoon, your artistic skill has brought an indispensible dimensionality to our story … and to Rescue's jowls. Your illustrations bring out the child in all of us. It is an honour to have made this book with you, given our families' experiences on 15/4/13. Cathy Zemaitis and Currahee, your presence in our lives has been life-changing. Thank you to Christy Bassett, Sharron Kahn Luttrell, Rescue's inmate handler, and the entire NEADS staff for making Rescue the incredible service dog and best friend that he is. Thank you to Cindy and Bob Lepofsky, Mike and Susan Curtin, Brownstone Insurance, and all NEADS supporters who make so many amazing service dogs possible. To our parents and siblings, for wholeheartedly embracing Rescue and for travelling this long road with us. To all of our friends and their service dog companions who have helped us cherish life and its many blessings. To the rest of our family and friends, thank you for making our causes your own. To the countless children who are just as captivated by Rescue as we are, and whose genuine curiosity taught us that we are born with acceptance in our hearts. And to Rescue, thank you for all the many ways you make us laugh, comfort us, and accompany us on life's journey. You brighten every day.

Jessica Kensky & Patrick Downes
Cambridge, Massachusetts, USA
2017

PHOTO CREDIT: KYLA DUNLAVEY / NO. 7 PHOTOGRAPHY

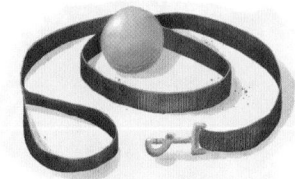

*For all of those who have supported us through our obstacles
and to honour those who are going through their own*

Never forget: M. R., K. C., L. L., S. C.

~ J. & P. & R.

For Jessica, Patrick & Rescue
~ S. M.

First published 2018 by Walker Books Ltd
87 Vauxhall Walk, London SE11 5HJ

2 4 6 8 10 9 7 5 3 1

Text © 2018 Jessica Kensky and Patrick Downes
Illustrations © 2018 Scott Magoon

The right of Jessica Kensky and Patrick Downes, and of Scott Magoon to be identified as authors and illustrator respectively
of this work has been asserted by them in accordance with the Copyright, Designs and Patents Act 1988

This book has been typeset in New Century Schoolbook

Printed in China

British Library Cataloguing in Publication Data:
a catalogue record for this book is available from the British Library

ISBN 978-1-4063-8046-0

www.walker.co.uk